SIMPLE MACHINES

SCREWS

Nancy Dickmann

BROWN BEAR BOOKS

Published by Brown Bear Books Ltd
4877 N. Circulo Bujia
Tucson, AZ 85718
USA

and

Leroy House
436 Essex Rd
London N1 3QP
UK

ISBN 978-1-78121-401-5 (library bound)
ISBN 978-1-78121-431-2 (paperback)

Library of Congress Cataloging-in-Publication Data available on request

Text: Nancy Dickmann
Design Manager: Keith Davis
Picture Manger: Sophie Mortimer
Editorial Director: Lindsey Lowe
Children's Publisher: Anne O'Daly

Manufactured in the United States of America
CPSIA compliance information: Batch#AG/5608

Picture Credits
The photographs in this book are used by permission and through the courtesy of:

Front Cover: Dreamstime: Stephen Mcsweeny main; Shutterstock: bl.
Interior: Alamy: Patrick Guenette 12, Paul Mayall Italy 12–13; Dreamstime: Valentin Armianu 20–21, Kurhan 6–7, Stephen Mcsweeny 14, Seoterra 6, Olena Yakobchuk 9; Public Domain: 15cr; Shutterstock: 1, 11, 17tr, 20r, 21b, Suzanne Tucker 10; Thinkstock: istockphoto 4, 4–5, 8–9, 10–11, 14–15, 15b, 16, 16–17, 18–19.

All other artwork and photography © Brown Bear Books.

t-top, r-right, l-left, c-center, b-bottom

Brown Bear Books has made every attempt to contact the copyright holder. If you have any information please contact: licensing@brownbearbooks.co.uk

Websites
The website addresses in this book were valid at the time of going to press. However, it is possible that contents or addresses may change following publication of this book. No responsibility for any such changes can be accepted by the author or the publisher. Readers should be supervised when they access the Internet.

Words in **bold** appear in the Useful Words on page 23.

Contents

What Is a Screw?

You have probably seen screws. They are used to join pieces of wood together. But there are many other types of screws. They all have the same basic shape. And they all do the same jobs.

Screws come in all sizes, from tiny to enormous.

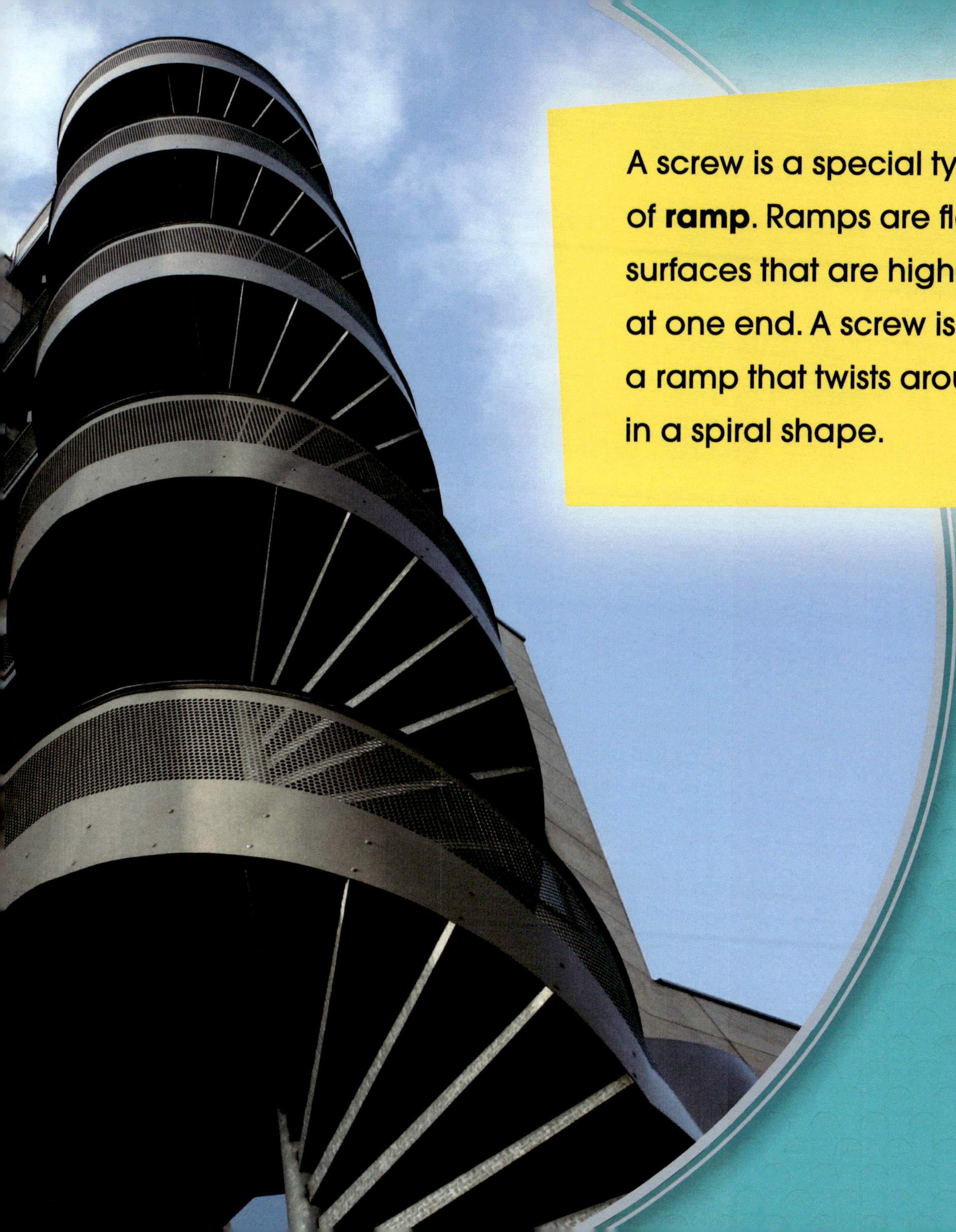

A screw is a special type of **ramp**. Ramps are flat surfaces that are higher at one end. A screw is a ramp that twists around in a spiral shape.

What Are Machines?

Machines are all around us. They help us do work. A **machine** like a screw can help lift things. It can also fasten them together. Some machines make the **force** we use more powerful.

WOW!

Many everyday objects are machines. An electric drill is a complicated machine. Its bit is a simple screw.

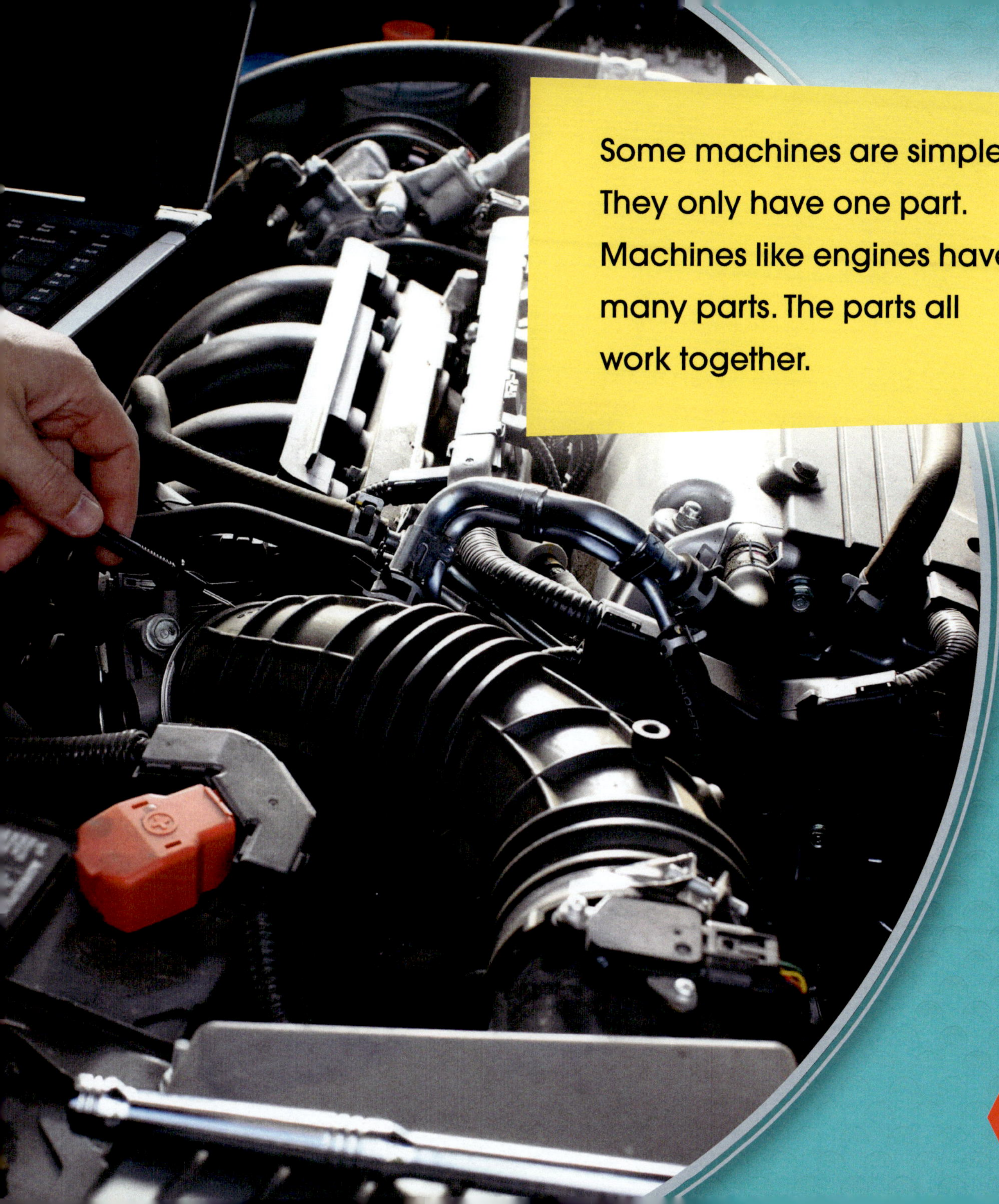

Some machines are simple. They only have one part. Machines like engines have many parts. The parts all work together.

Screws and Forces

A **force** is a push or pull. Screws change a force's direction. They take a force that goes around and around. They change it into one that goes up and down.

Threads

A screw has ridges and grooves. They are called threads.

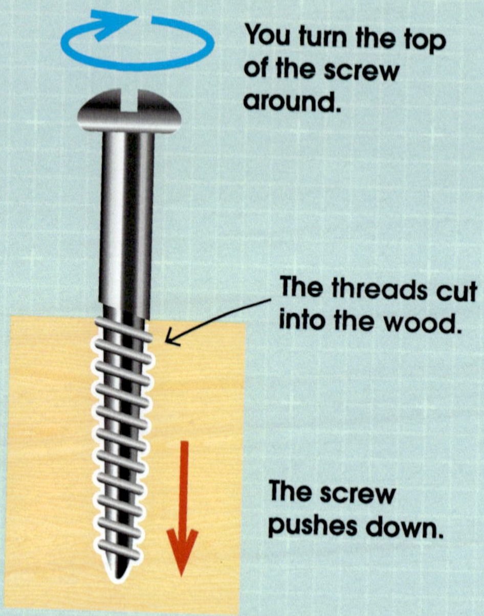

Hammering a nail is hard work. You need less force to turn a screw. Your work is easier, but you have to work for longer.

Holding Things Together

Screws can hold things together. The **threads** bite deep into wood. A long screw can hold pieces of wood together. It would take a lot of **force** to pull them apart.

WOW!

A jar has a screw at the top. It fits into threads inside the lid. The threads hold the lid on tight.

Some screws fit into a nut. The inside of the nut has threads. They match the threads on the screw. The two pieces screw tightly together.

Screws in the Past

People have used screws for a long time. The Greeks used them to water crops. They put a screw inside a pipe. They put the bottom end in water. Then they turned the screw. It raised the water.

The screw turns. This makes water come out at the top of the pipe.

Screws were used in a **press**. Turning the screw made a heavy weight push down. It could crush olives to release oil. It could crush apples to make cider.

WOW!

A screw press could also print books. It pressed letters down onto paper.

Screws Today

Screws do different jobs. An auger uses a screw. Big augers dig into the ground. Their screws turn to push into the soil. They bring the soil up to the surface.

Fishers use augers to reach the water below the ice.

WOW!

A screw turbine goes in a river. Water flows past it. This makes the turbine turn. The turbine provides power to homes.

Many bridges use steel bolts. Bolts have **threads**. They screw tightly into a nut. Rows of bolts hold a bridge together.

Screws at Home

There are screws in your home.
An outside faucet has **threads**.
You can screw a hose onto it.
The threads fit together.
They make a seal so
water cannot leak out.

WOW!

A lightbulb has a metal screw. It screws into the fixture. The threads hold the lightbulb in place.

Bicycle tires have a valve for adding air. The valve has threads at the end. You screw a lid onto them.

Compound Machines

Screws are simple machines. So are levers and wedges. We can join them together. They form a **compound machine**. All the parts work together.

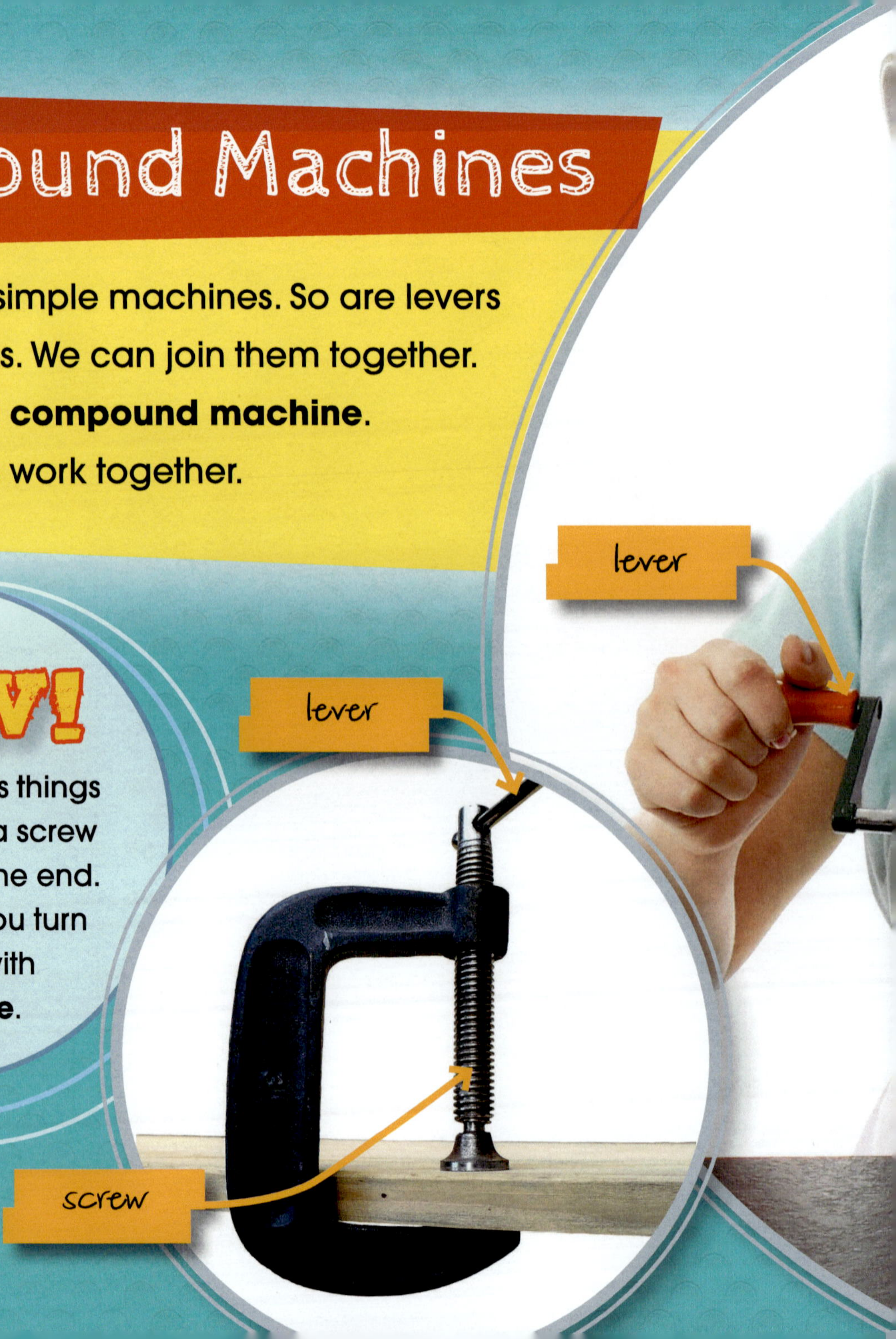

WOW!

A C-clamp holds things in place. It has a screw with a **lever** at the end. The lever lets you turn the screw with more **force**.

This **machine** peels apples. It is made of simple machines. A long screw pokes into the apple. A lever helps turn the screw. It pushes the apple against a **wedge**. The wedge cuts into the peel.

Spot the Screw!

Can you find the screws in these pictures?

1

2

3

5

4

Try It!

A screw is a special type of ramp. But how can a ramp turn into a screw?

You will need:

- piece of paper
- pencil
- marker or crayon
- ruler
- scissors
- tape

1. Use your ruler to draw a diagonal line from one corner of the paper to another.

2. Cut along the line. You should have a triangle. This is the shape of a ramp. Color a narrow line along the edge you cut.

4. Tape an uncolored edge to the pencil.

5. Wrap the paper around the pencil. Keep wrapping until you have used it all.

6. Tape off the end.

Can you see how the paper wraps around in a spiral shape? Your ramp has turned into a screw!

Useful Words

compound machine A machine that is made up of smaller machines. It can have several different simple machines.

force A push or a pull.

lever Type of simple machine. A lever has a long beam that rests on a point called a pivot.

machine Something that helps us do work. Machines use energy to do a job.

press A machine that uses a screw to push a weight down. Presses can be used to crush things.

ramp A flat surface that is higher at one end. Ramps can help lift heavy objects.

threads Grooves and ridges that go around a screw.

wedge A simple machine with angled sides. Wedges can split things apart.

Answers to page 20–21: Did you spot the screws? **1.** The C-clamp; **2.** the drill's bit; **3.** the spiral staircase; **4.** the base of the lightbulb; **5.** the threaded bolts.

Find out More

Websites

www.idahoptv.org/sciencetrek/topics/simple_machines/facts.cfm

www.msichicago.org/play/simplemachines/

www.scienceforkidsclub.com/simple-machines.html

Books

Going Ice Fishing: Lever vs. Screw Mari Schuh, Lerner Publishing, 2015

Screws in Action Gillian Gosman, PowerKids Press 2010

Screws, Nuts, and Bolts Sian Smith, Heinemann Raintree 2012

Index